Rocket
Has a Sleepover

Copyright © 2021 by Tad Hills
Text by Elle Stephens
Art by Grace Mills

All rights reserved. Published in the United States by Random House Studio, an imprint of
Random House Children's Books, a division of Penguin Random House LLC, New York.

Random House Studio and the colophon are registered trademarks of Penguin Random House LLC.

Visit us on the Web!
rhcbooks.com

Educators and librarians, for a variety of teaching tools, visit us at RHTeachersLibrarians.com

Library of Congress Cataloging-in-Publication Data is available upon request.
ISBN 978-0-593-18125-6 (hardcover) — ISBN 978-0-593-18122-5 (trade pbk.) —
ISBN 978-0-593-18123-2 (lib. bdg.) — ISBN 978-0-593-18124-9 (ebook)

The text of this book is set in 28-point Century.
The illustrations were digitally rendered.

MANUFACTURED IN CHINA
10 9 8 7 6 5 4 3 2 1

First Edition

Rocket
Has a Sleepover

Pictures based on the art by Tad Hills

RANDOM HOUSE STUDIO ⌂ NEW YORK

Rocket is happy!

He is having a sleepover
with his friends.

The friends play
hide-and-seek.

They eat snacks.

Later,
they say
good night.

But Rocket
is not tired.
He can not sleep.

"I will tell you a story," says Fred.

"There once was a puppy
who loved to swim."

"One day,

he met a frog."

"Then what?"
asks Rocket.

Fred falls asleep!

Rocket is not tired.
"I will finish the story,"
says Owl.

"The puppy and the frog had a race."

"Who won?" asks Rocket.

Zzzzz . . .

Now Owl is
asleep!

Rocket is not tired.

"I will finish
the story,"
says Bella.

"The frog got tired and needed to rest!" says Bella.

"The frog called
for help."

"Then what?"
asks Rocket.

Now Bella
is asleep!

"Oh no," says Rocket.
All his friends
are asleep.

"I will finish
the story,"
he says.

"The puppy
went back."

"He helped the frog."

"They finished
the race together,"
says Rocket.

"The frog and the puppy were tired."
Rocket yawns.

"They found a blanket
and fell fast asleep.
The end."

Rocket is tired.

He falls fast asleep.

The end.